JOAN W. BLOS

Lottie's CIRCUS

ILLUSTRATED BY IRENE TRIVAS

MORROW JUNIOR BOOKS / NEW YORK

Text copyright © 1989 by Joan W. Blos
Illustrations copyright © 1989 by Irene Trivas
Printed in the United States of America.
1 2 3 4 5 6 7 8 9 10
Library of Congress Cataloging-in-Publication Data
Blos, Joan W.
Lottie's circus / by Joan W. Blos : illustrated by Irene Trivas.
p.   cm.
Summary: Lottie imagines that she and her cat, Famous, are the
stars of a wonderful circus.
ISBN 0-688-06746-8—ISBN 0-688-06747-6 (lib. bdg.)
[1. Imagination—Fiction. 2. Circus—Fiction. 3. Cats—Fiction.]
I. Trivas, Irene, ill. II. Title.
PZ7.B6237Lo 1989
[E]—dc19   88-39035   CIP   AC

Lottie's CIRCUS

Every time she reads a story
to her cat who listens while he purrs,

Lottie must explain again
that magic is like wishing.
"First you make-believe," she says,
"and then something special happens."

At the circus ticket office
a restless crowd is waiting.

Lottie entertains them
with a difficult magic trick.

Then she has to blow up the balloons

and get the popcorn popping.

There are seats to build

and signs to paint.

Toes pressed down
in her mother's high-heeled shoes,
Lottie, the World's Tallest Lady,
welcomes one and all.

Lottie lets the people know
what food there is to buy.
"Hot dogs! Lemonade! Step right up!
Best you ever tasted, just fifty cents a cup."

While the clowns put on their clown suits,

the animals practice their tricks.

Lottie is not afraid to make
the largest lion roar.

As Lottie drives the calliope,
music blares out for the march,
and the circus show begins!

Now there comes the most exciting part!
"Ladies and gentlemen,
　　watch this act
　　　　of the one and only
　　　　　　Famous Cat—
　　　　　　　　Famous, you come back!"

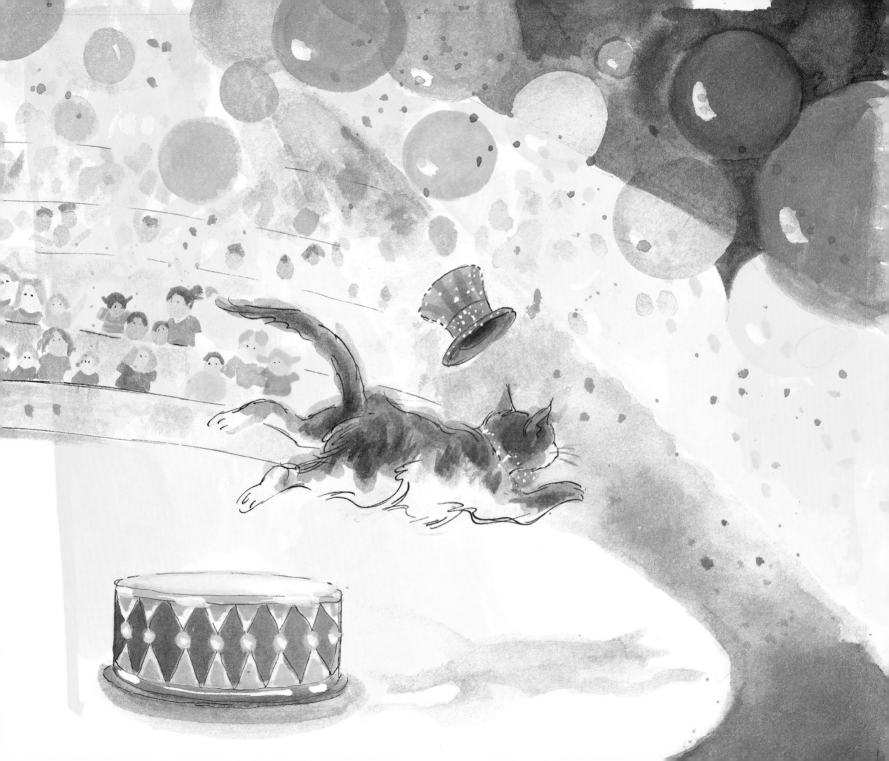

"Next time," Lottie promises, "it will be
an even bigger circus."
Famous flicks his tail.

For supper they have
hamburgers and spaghetti
and ice-cold lemonade.

Holding Famous close to her,
Lottie sits on her father's lap
while he reads a story.
That way she can turn the pages
all the way to—
The End.